INDIAN TWO FEET
and the
ABC MOOSE HUNT

83143

By Margaret Friskey

Illustrated by John Hawkinson

CHILDRENS PRESS, CHICAGO

Library of Congress Cataloging in Publication Data

Friskey, Margaret, 1901-
  Indian Two Feet and the ABC moose hunt.

  SUMMARY: A young Indian goes hunting for his first moose.
  [1. Indians of North America—Fiction. 2. Stories
in rhyme. 3. Alphabet books] I. Hawkinson, John,
1912- II. Title.
PZ8.3.F9179In   [E]   77-4467
ISBN 0-516-03500-2

4 5 6 7 8 9 10 11 12 R 85 84 83 82 81 80

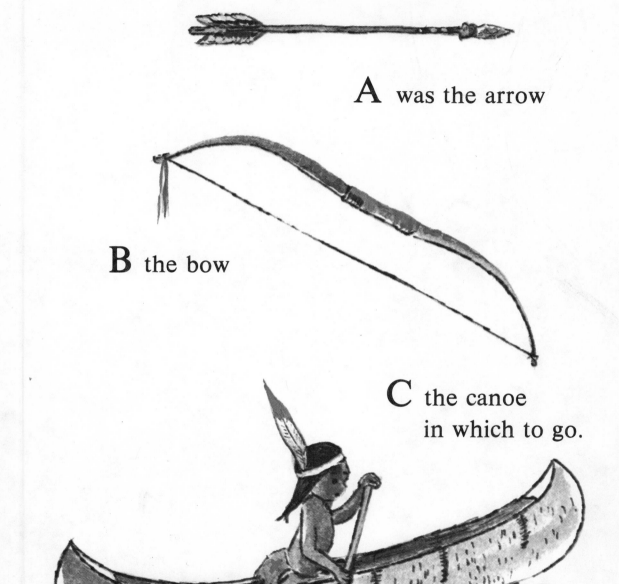

A was the arrow

B the bow

C the canoe
in which to go.

D was the ducklings diving deep.

E   an eagle looking on.

F a funny frightened fawn.

G for going like a goose.

H for hunting
  for a moose.

I the Indian
    left his tent.

J the journey
on which he went.

K for the kits
of the old gray fox.

L for lizards
on the rocks.

M was the moose
　　　as big as a mountain.

N was for nearer
and nearer he drew.

O was for oops!
Over went the canoe.

P was the paddle
  that floated aside.

Q was the quail
that hopped on for a ride.

R a raccoon
was eating a clam.

S was the swimming
that Two Feet swam.

T was for Two Feet
and trouble, too.

Gone was the
arrow
the bow
the canoe.

U up a hillside
    went Two Feet to see

V the village
    where he ought to be.

W wise were the old ones
 who waited and cried,
 "Good for you Two Feet.
 You missed but you tried."

X was his mark
 on the side of the teepee.
 No moose picture yet,
 But someday there might be.

Y "Yes, you are young yet,"
the old ones agreed.
"Another year older
and you might succeed."

However:

Z was for zero
for none and for naught.
That is how many
moose were caught.

A a   B b   C c   D d   E e

F f   G g   H h   I i   J j

K k   L l   M m   N n   O o

P p   Q q   R r   S s   T t

U u   V v   W w   X x   Y y

Z z